TO *Tenisha Diane Brown*

DISNEY'S
SMALL WORLD LIBRARY
DONALD'S FANTASTIC FIESTA
An Adventure in Mexico

GROLIER ENTERPRISES INC.
DANBURY, CONNECTICUT

© The Walt Disney Company. All rights reserved.
Printed in the United States of America.
Developed by The Walt Disney Company in conjunction with Nancy Hall, Inc.
ISBN 0-7172-8216-3

"Stop here!" cried Donald to the taxi driver. "There are our friends!"

He paid the fare and jumped out after Grandma Duck, Daisy, Huey, Dewey, and Louie.

"Welcome to Mexico!" said Pablo and Rosa.

The whole group went into the house, where Pablo
and Rosa's mother had a huge meal waiting for them.

"It's so good to see you all again," said Mrs. Perez.
"And just wait till you see all the wonderful things we
have planned for you to do."

Donald smiled happily. Tomorrow was his birthday,
and he was sure everyone was planning a big celebration
for him.

The next morning Donald woke up in a wonderful mood.

"Happy birthday to me, happy birthday to me," sang Donald.

"Yes, siree, the birthday boy sure looks spiffy today," he said to his reflection in the mirror.

Then Donald bounded down the stairs, two at a time. "I don't want to keep everyone waiting," he thought. "They probably can't wait to wish me a happy birthday."

But when he got to the breakfast table, all he heard was *"Buenos días,"* which means "good morning" in Spanish, the language that is spoken in Mexico. Worse still, everyone had already made plans for the day, and none of the plans included Donald.

Daisy was going to have a cooking lesson from Mrs. Perez, and Pablo was planning to teach her and the nephews how to play jai alai, which he told them was a game like handball.

"What about me?" thought Donald sadly. "Doesn't anyone remember what day it is?"

Grandma turned to Donald. "Rosa has offered to take me on a tour of Mexico City," said Grandma. "Would you like to come with us?"

"Sure, why not?" said Donald, brightening.

Donald smiled as a pleasant thought occurred to him. "Now I get it," he said to himself. "Everybody else is staying home to plan a surprise party for me, and they want to get me out of the house!"

Donald jumped up from the table. "What time do we leave?" he asked enthusiastically.

"Let's go get the bus right away," said Rosa. "That way we'll have plenty of time to see everything."

"First stop, the Floating Gardens," called the bus driver.

"Floating gardens?" asked Grandma in disbelief. "I've never heard of a garden that floats!"

"Follow me," said Rosa as she headed for the ticket office. Rosa bought three tickets, and before long they were drifting on the water in a flower-filled boat.

"Many years ago, the Aztec Indians planted vegetables and flowers on wooden rafts that floated in the shallow water," explained Rosa. "People come from all over the world to admire the flowers that still grow here."

"They certainly are beautiful," agreed Grandma.

A moment later another boat floated by. A band was playing lively music on board.

"Do you know how to play 'Happy Birthday?'" called Donald. But no one heard him above the music.

After their boat ride, the three sightseers got back on the bus. Soon they were driving through Mexico City, Mexico's beautiful capital.

"To your left, you will see the National Palace," instructed the tour guide. "It was built on the ruins of an Aztec temple by a Spanish explorer named Cortés. Many hundreds of years ago, Mexico was a land of enormous temples and palaces. Aztec emperors, like Montezuma II, lived here in splendor."

"I wonder how the Aztecs would have celebrated Montezuma's birthday," muttered Donald. "I bet he had lots of candles on his cake!"

"Next stop is Chapultepec Park," called the bus driver.

"Then we can go visit the National Museum of Anthropology," said Rosa.

Outside the museum, Grandma pointed to an enormous statue.

"My goodness!" she exclaimed. "What's that?"

"That's Tlaloc," replied Rosa, "the Aztec rain god. The statue weighs eighty tons. It took a giant truck with twenty wheels to get it here from the site where it was built. The summer it was brought here, there had been a terrible drought, with no rain for weeks and weeks. As soon as the statue was removed from the truck, a big thunderstorm soaked the city with much-needed rain."

"What a wonderful story!" said Grandma.

"Yes," agreed Donald, whose attention had turned to
a clock on the wall that reminded him that it was getting
late. "Shouldn't we be getting back home now?"

Grandma agreed, but when they left the museum the day was so beautiful that she couldn't resist taking a stroll through the park.

"Look!" cried Rosa. "There's a mime! That's an actor who doesn't speak," she explained to Donald and Grandma.

Rosa, Grandma, and Donald joined the group that had formed around the mime. Donald laughed as the mime pretended to sew his fingers together. Then Donald started to get a little nervous. What if they started his birthday party at home without him?

"Maybe if I do a pantomime of my own, they'll get the hint," Donald thought to himself.

First he pretended to open some presents. Next he blew out the candles on an imaginary birthday cake. But Grandma wasn't paying attention to Donald.

"While we're here, why don't we visit the zoo?" suggested Rosa.

"Oh, yes," said Grandma. "We must go see the pandas."

Donald sighed. "Maybe they really did forget my birthday after all," he thought.

But as they approached the panda exhibit, they heard a group of people singing "Happy Birthday."

ZOOLÓGICO DE CHAPULTEPEC

"Maybe my surprise party is going to be right here!" Donald said to himself.

Donald arrived just in time to see some school children presenting one of the baby pandas with a birthday cake. "At least someone is having a birthday party," said Donald under his breath. Then he pleaded with Grandma to head home.

"Yes, I guess we should be going," said Grandma. But as they headed back they passed a beautiful street called El Paseo de la Reforma.

Soon they were wandering in and out of store after store. Grandma bought a lovely hand-woven shawl and a pottery pie plate.

"I better get myself some birthday presents, just in case," Donald thought, as he wrapped himself in a colorful serape and put a huge sombrero on his head.

He paid for his presents to himself just as the stores were closing.

"Now it's siesta time," explained Rosa. "Let's call it a day and go home for some rest."

Donald agreed enthusiastically, and they all boarded the bus for home.

On the way home, Rosa pointed out some more sights along the way.

"There's the University of Mexico Library over there," she said, pointing to a spectacular building.

"It's beautiful!" exclaimed Donald. "It must have taken a long time to paint so many colors."

"The building is not painted," replied Rosa. "The colors you see are a mosaic, made up of seven million stone chips."

When they got home, the house was quiet.

"Sshhh," whispered Grandma. "Everyone is sleeping. I think I'll take a siesta, too."

"Me, too," yawned Rosa.

Donald waited until they were out of sight. Then he began to snoop around the house looking for signs of his birthday party. First he went into the living room to look for party decorations. All he saw was a big papier mâché donkey hanging from the ceiling and a large hat lying on the floor. Donald looked in the closet and under the furniture, but he still didn't see one present.

Next Donald went into the kitchen to look for his birthday cake, but the only thing he found was a great big box. He peeked inside.

"Pancakes!" he snorted, stamping his foot. "It looks like there's not going to be a party after all." Donald sighed sadly. "I guess I might as well take a nap, too."

When Donald woke up, he was in a terrible mood.

"Some birthday!" he griped. "I'm not even going to tell them it was my birthday until tomorrow. Then they'll be sorry they forgot about me!"

Donald went into the living room and, with a heavy sigh, plopped himself into a chair.

"Surprise!" everyone shouted, jumping out from behind the door and the furniture.

"Now you're going to find out how we celebrate birthdays in my country," declared Pablo. "It's time to break the piñata."

Tying a blindfold around Donald's eyes, Pablo pulled
him under the donkey hanging from the ceiling. Then he
handed Donald a long stick.

"Hit the piñata as hard as you can," Pablo instructed.

Donald did as he was told.

"Good job!" cried Pablo. "You cracked it!"

Then everyone else took a turn hitting the piñata until
it split open, showering them all with presents and candy.

"Oh, boy!" exclaimed Donald, scrambling to fill up his
pockets.

Then Pablo picked up his guitar and began to play a lively tune. Taking her guests by the hands, Rosa taught everyone to do the Mexican Hat Dance.

When they were finished dancing, Mrs. Perez and Daisy came out of the kitchen carrying a platter. On it were the pancakes that Donald had seen in the big box. But now they were filled with a delicious mixture of meat, cheese, and spices.

"These are tacos and enchiladas," said Daisy proudly. "We made them today."

Donald beamed as everyone sang him the Mexican birthday song called "Las Mañanitas."

"This is the best birthday I've ever had!" cried Donald.

Did You Know...?

There are many different customs and places that make each country special. Do you remember some of the things below from the story?

Mexico City is the capital city of Mexico. At an altitude of 7,349 feet, it is one of the highest cities in the world. It is also the second most populated city in the world, after Shanghai, China.

The Paseo de la Reforma in Mexico City is lined with trees and has seven landscaped intersections. It is considered one of the most beautiful avenues in the world.

A favorite sport in Mexico is jai alai, which is similar to the game of handball. Players scoop a rubber ball into a basketlike racket and then hurl it against a wall. The ball moves so quickly that jai alai is sometimes called the fastest game in the world.

Chapultepec Park, in Mexico City, has something for everyone. Besides lakes, trees, and a zoo, it also has an amusement park that contains one of the world's tallest and scariest roller coasters.

The Aztecs lived in Mexico long ago. They built many tall pyramids that can still be seen today.

Siestas are a way of life in Mexico. Most businesses close for two hours or more during the hottest part of the afternoon. People go home to eat, rest, and be with their families.

Mexican children get to celebrate
their birthdays two days each year.
One day is their actual birthday.
The other day is the feast day of
the saint after whom they are
named.

Piñatas are made of either papier mâché or pottery,
and are usually in the shape of a donkey, bull, or other
animal. *Piñatas* are filled with candy, fruit, and toys, and
children try to break them with sticks while blindfolded.
They are a part of Christmas and Easter celebrations,
as well as birthdays.

Spanish is the language
spoken in Mexico. *Adios, amigos*
(ah-dee-OSE ah-ME-gose) means
"good-bye, friends"
in Spanish.

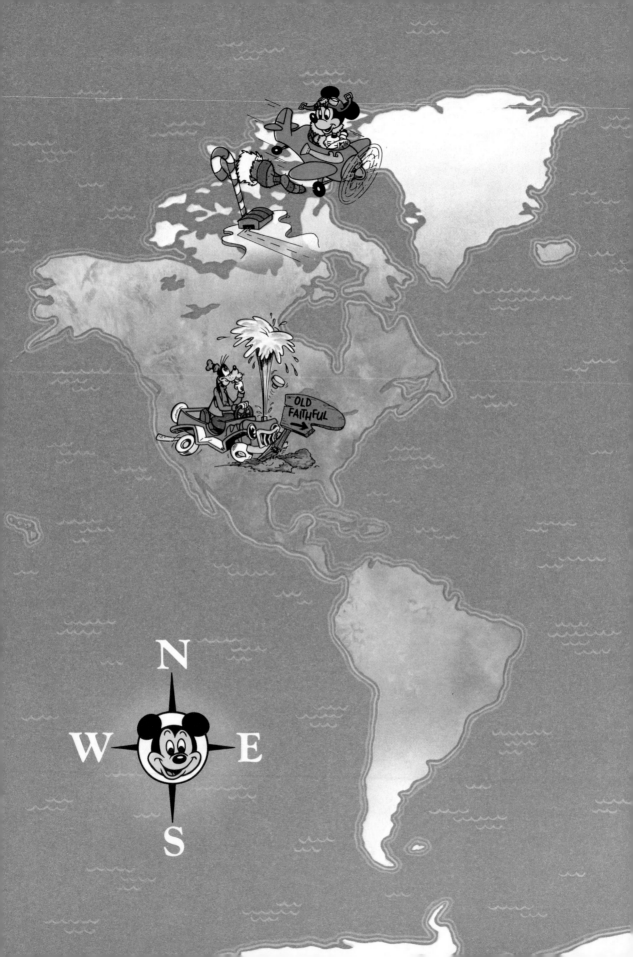